Also by
Donald W. Kruse

Spinosaur Island

No one is safe from the
terrifying monsters and their
BONE CRUSHING

JAWS!!

WHISKERS

So You Think
It's Safe to Swim in the Lake?

THINK AGAIN!

THE GHOST
OF WOLVERINE FOREST

The Ghost
of
Wolverine
Forest

Donald W. Kruse

ZACCHEUS ENTERTAINMENT
Minong, WI

The Ghost of Wolverine Forest

by Donald W. Kruse is published by:

ZACCHEUS ENTERTAINMENT

The Ghost of Wolverine Forest

Copyright © 2019 by Donald W. Kruse

Zaccheus Entertainment
P.O. Box 23
Minong, WI 54859

ISBN: 978-0-9994571-5-3

1st Edition copyright 2009
2nd Edition copyright 2019

Cover and interior illustrations by Craig Howarth

Manufactured in the United States of America

A special thank you from the author to Craig Howarth.

To

Stephen King

one of my

favorite authors

and who

unwittingly

inspired me to

write a

SCARY story!

ACKNOWLEDGMENTS

I thank God for the gift of writing. And, a very special thank you to Ms. Phyllis Diller, who taught me, "Onward and Upward!" I love you, my lady.

THIRTY STEPS. That's all it takes to get lost in Wolverine Forest.

The woods are so thick, so vast, that once you go in, you may *never* come out. Some places are so thick with twisted vines and thorny bushes, you couldn't hack your way out with a machete. You could hack off a man's arm before you could cut through *that* tangled mess. And no one would hear his screams.

Huge trees of all kinds jut up from the moss-covered forest floor. Their thick branches form a leafy roof, blocking out most of the sunlight. This keeps the forest below cool, damp ... and dark.

Very, very ... dark.

It's so dark, you couldn't see a deer standing fifty feet in front of you. Not that the deer would have long to live, anyway.

Because it wouldn't—not if the man-eating creature, lurking in the woods, ever caught whiff of the deer's scent.

*J*ust like what happened to little Tommy Hansen twenty years ago. He was foolish enough to enter these woods, and he never came out … alive. All the police ever found were his bones … and his camera.

Apparently Tommy had been out hiking and taking pictures of animals. When the police had developed his film, there were several photographs of birds, squirrels, rabbits, and deer. And one photo of the creature—just before it had attacked.

Tommy wouldn't have had time to take more than one picture. The police say the creature would've been on him in an instant, with its bone-crushing jaws, gnashing teeth, and razor-sharp claws. Poor Tommy Hansen never had a chance. Deep inside the woods, he had been all alone and helpless. No one would have heard his screams.

The death of Tommy Hansen was disturbing enough, but that wasn't all. In the photo of the creature, one can see an old, haggard woman, dressed in black, standing behind the creature, watching it close in on Tommy. But instead of having a look of alarm on her face, the old woman ... is smiling.

The police think the old woman is a witch, and the creature is her pet, trained to kill anyone who wanders into Wolverine Forest. But the police have never been able to find her, or the creature. They even flew over the forest in airplanes and helicopters. And they brought in dozens of dogs specially trained in hunting and tracking. And hundreds of volunteers searched the woods. But in the end, they found nothing. And for the last twenty years, there has been no sign of the old woman or her creature.

Until now ...

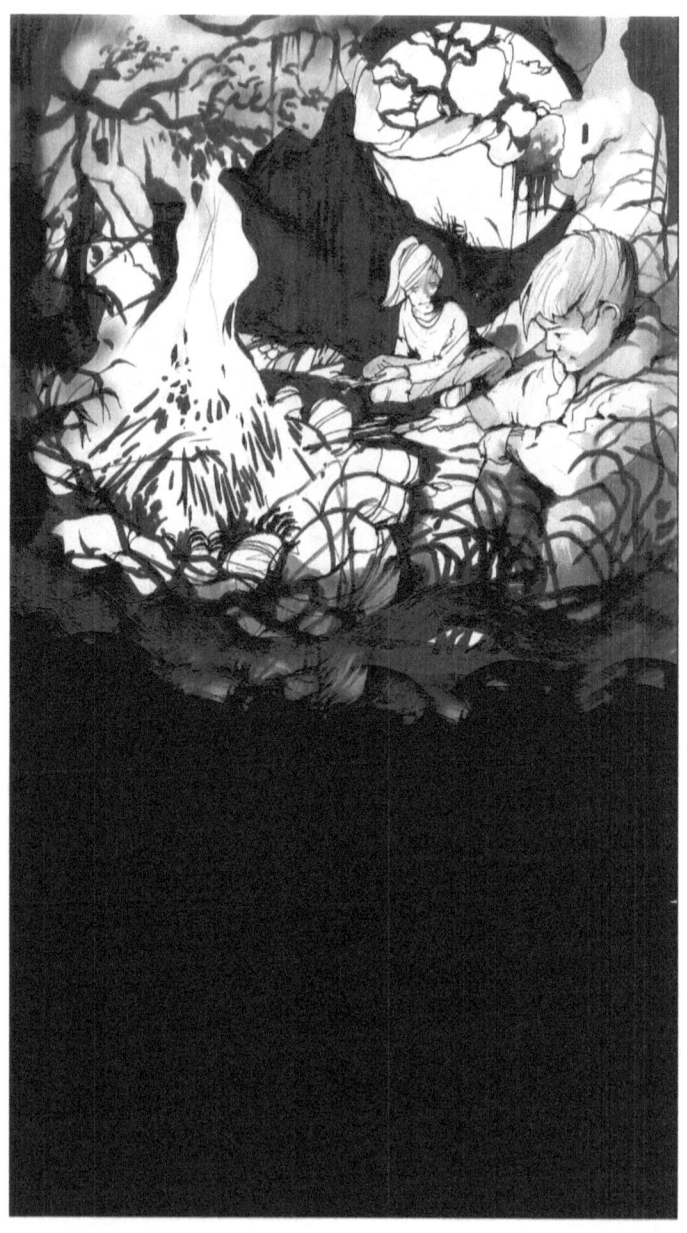

"It wasn't *my* idea to take a shortcut," said eleven-year-old Sarah, shivering in the late September breeze. It was Saturday afternoon, and the warm, sunny morning had turned into a cloudy, chilly day. Sarah stood over her eleven-year-old friend, Brad, watching him start a campfire with siphoned gasoline from his all terrain vehicle, or quad.

"Don't panic," Brad said, placing dead sticks on the growing fire. "Worse-case scenario—we'll have to spend the night if nobody finds us before dark. No big deal. At least we got a campfire. We won't freeze."

"Spend the night! Are you nuts!" Sarah cried, hugging herself tightly. "What about the ghost? They say these woods are haunted!"

Brad broke a dead branch across his knee and placed the wood on his fire. "Ah, excuse me ... we're in the sixth grade, right?"

"So what?" Sarah asked, rubbing her arms and stamping her feet.

"So we're old enough to know that there are no such things as ghosts."

"Oh, yeah?" said Sarah. "Well, try telling that to Tommy Hansen's family."

Brad snapped another dead branch over his knee and added the wood to the fire. The flames danced and flickered, reaching higher and higher, and growing warmer by the minute. "Tommy Hansen was killed by a wild animal—probably some kind of wolf—not a ghost."

"A wolf!" Sarah cried. "That wasn't a wolf in the picture they found. And what about the old woman in the picture. Some say she's an evil witch. If these woods aren't haunted, then why did your quad die out? And how come both of our cell phones are suddenly dead? Just a coincidence? I think not."

*A*s the fire grew bigger, the day grew shorter ... and darker. The red, orange, and yellow leaves of autumn had flashed vibrantly in that morning's radiant sunshine. But now they were mere shadows fluttering in the evening breeze. Soon the waning daylight slipped into darkness, enveloping Brad and Sarah, and the surrounding woods.

"My parents will be worried sick," said Sarah, huddled next to Brad on a log in front of the fire. "I'm in big trouble when they find us."

Suddenly ...

everything got very, very quiet.
The breeze stopped dead, the leaves
stopped fluttering, and the flames
died down ... to a flicker.

"What's going on, Brad?" Sarah asked, squeezing his arm.

But before he could answer, a voice whispered through the trees …

"Go back!"

A burst of goosebumps tingled down Sarah's spine. She felt Brad tense as she buried her face in his chest. "Brad, who is it?" she cried, trembling.

Brad jumped up to face the voice. "Who's there?" he yelled.

But no one answered. Only stillness. Dead quiet.

And then ...

… the voice, whispering again. "Leave these woods at once!"

Sarah sprang to her feet, threw herself at Brad, clinging to him, and screamed, "Brad, let's get out of here!"

Suddenly a twig snapped in the darkness, just outside the fire's light. And then the sound of footsteps began … one after the other … step by step. Getting closer. Closer.

Closer ...

Terrified, Brad and Sarah clung to each other, straining to see the intruder. But there was no one there. Only the sound of the approaching footsteps.

And then it happened ... a ghost appeared right before their eyes. It was little Tommy Hansen, torn to pieces and covered with blood. Yet, he appeared to be in no pain—not anymore. For *this* Tommy Hansen ...

was dead.

Brad and Sarah shook with fear. Tears streamed down Sarah's cheeks, she was so scared. Brad felt his knees turn to rubber, and his throat tightened up like a knot. He tried to speak, but his voice trembled so badly, it sounded like he might start to cry, too.

But he didn't. Instead, he stepped in front of Sarah, protecting her, cleared his throat and asked, "What do you want?"

"My name is Tommy Hansen. I am the ghost of Wolverine Forest. You already know how I died. When I was only eight-years-old, I was killed by the beast, Cytok. But what you didn't know is that Cytok roams these woods, hunting and killing animals for his master, the witch, to eat. Her name is Zeena, and she and Cytok have been living in these woods for hundreds of years. There used to be two creatures—Cytok had a mate whose name was Tusks. I don't know which one was the girl creature and which one was the boy creature. All I know is Tusks died recently when he or she fell into a saltwater pond deep inside the woods. Zeena, Cytok, and Tusks are all demons.

Nothing can destroy them, except …

... salt water."

Brad cleared his throat again, then asked, "But why did they want to kill *you?* Zeena didn't eat you, and you certainly were no threat to her—*you* couldn't harm her. You were just a little kid."

"Zeena has a secret that she wants kept hidden forever. Almost two hundred years ago, the town of Wolverine was just beginning. A few dozen farmers and fur traders started the town with their families. They all worked very hard every day, building houses, farms, and stores. It took them many years to build the town, and they finally had everything they needed … except a school. So after many more years of working hard and saving their money, the settlers were finally able to save up enough silver and gold to build a school."

"Wolverine had a school?" asked Sarah, feeling less afraid now. "But the town of Wolverine has never had a school. Even now, we have to take a bus to Taylorville to go to school."

"That's right," said the ghost. "Thanks to Zeena, who stole the settlers' silver and gold, the school was never built, and the money has never been found."

"Do you know where it is?" Brad asked, getting excited at the thought of all that money.

"Yes, I do," replied the ghost. "Zeena keeps it in a wooden chest under the floor boards of her underground hut."

"Maybe we can get it back!" cried Brad, his heart beating a little faster.

"Wait a minute," Sarah said. "Who's we? If you think I'm going near that witch's house, you're crazy!"

"No!"

… said the ghost. "You mustn't go near there. You must leave these woods as soon as you can. It won't be long before Cytok smells you, hunts you down and kills you. Zeena won't allow anyone near her hut. She has cast a spell so anyone entering these woods will lose their way and die. Because Zeena and Cytok are demons, they have no scent. So no one can smell them, and no dogs can track them. That's why no one can ever find them. And her hut is well-hidden beneath the forest floor. To go there would be foolish … and dangerous."

"So I was right!" Sarah cried. "Zeena's spell *is* what killed our cell phones and the quad."

"Yes," said the ghost. "And she can easily kill both of you, as well."

"But, if I can figure out a way to destroy Zeena and Cytok first, then we'll be safe," Brad said, rubbing his chin. "And then you could take us to the treasure. We'll be rich!"

"Don't be nuts!" Sarah snapped. "You want to get us both killed? We have to get out of here before they even know we're here."

Suddenly ...

… the ghost rolled his eyes and moaned. He tilted his head upward toward the night sky, the whites of his eyes flashing in the firelight. Then he slowly lowered his head and stared directly at Brad and Sarah.

"They already know," he said.

"But, how?" Sarah asked, a knot forming in her stomach.

"Cytok has picked up your scent," said the ghost. "They're coming to get you."

"Then there's no escape, no way out," Brad said. "Is there?"

"No," said the ghost …

"You're doomed."

"Then we'll fight for our lives!" Brad cried. "If you'll help us, we can destroy them first!"

"Believe me," said the ghost, "I would like nothing more than to help you destroy Zeena and Cytok. For Zeena has cast a spell over me, so that my soul may never rest. It's my punishment for having taken a picture of her and her beast just before I died. The only way my spirit can be released from her spell is by destroying her."

"Then let's do it!" Brad said, clenching his fists.

"But, how?" the ghost asked.

"Lead us to the ...

saltwater pond,"

… Brad replied. "Quickly!"

Before Sarah could argue, Brad grabbed her hand, kicked the campfire out with dirt, then followed the ghost's voice through the moonlit forest.

Some time later, they came upon the saltwater pond. Stretching across the water was an old wooden bridge that arched upward in the middle. It had a railing on both sides, but after having tested it, Brad could tell the railings were old and weak. With hardly any effort at all, one could easily kick his way through them.

Hanging from treetops directly above the bridge were several thick vines. Brad tested these, too, and found that they were strong enough to hold him and Sarah when they swung on them. The trap was almost complete. Brad and Sarah were the bait. Now all they needed was their prey—Zeena and Cytok.

Brad and Sarah waited on the bridge. But they didn't have to wait long. "They're

coming!" the ghost warned. "They're almost here!"

Moments later Brad heard a rustling
noise in the underbrush along the pond's
shoreline.

And then ...

… Zeena and Cytok came into view beneath the full moon. Brad heard Sarah gasp with fright, and his own stomach churned when he saw the pure evil forms staring at him, waiting for him, at the foot of the bridge.

His heart pounding in his chest, Brad forced himself to speak in a loud, harsh tone.

"What are you waiting for, you creeps! Come and get us, if you got the guts!" Then Brad handed a vine to Sarah, and grabbed one for himself. "Jump when I say jump," he whispered. "And hang on as tight as you can!"

The old witch threw her head back and cackled. Then she glared at Brad and Sarah, her eyes big and fluid, and full of hate. "Cytok …

attack!"

The beast trampled across the bridge with lightning speed, its nostrils flared, teeth popping. It unleashed a bloodcurdling squeal, then lunged at Brad and Sarah.

Clutching the vines, Brad and Sarah launched themselves from the old, rickety railing, swinging out over the water and away from the bridge.

Cytok crashed through the railing, his teeth gnashing, his tusks glinting in the moonlight. He splashed into the pond with a horrible scream that could have awakened the dead. And then …

... he was gone.

few ripples lingered on the surface, shimmering under the full moon. Then … nothing.

"I'll kill you!" Zeena screamed, raising a dagger from her waistline. She charged the bridge, moving surprisingly, unnaturally fast for an old hag.

Sarah's vine was first to swing back to the bridge, right into Zeena's path. With one swift flick of her dagger, Zeena sliced through Sarah's vine, dropping Sarah back onto the bridge. The old witch bent over her, raised her dagger high into the air, and was just about to plunge it into Sarah's chest when …

WHAM!

Brad's vine came swinging back to the bridge just in time for him to kick the old hag as hard as he could.

Zeena screamed, dropped her dagger, then crashed through the opposite railing, and fell into the pond. Her screams were cut short, as the salt water bubbled and boiled around her, then finally gurgled over her head, completely dissolving her. A small cloud of steam wafted momentarily above the surface, then disappeared into the night air.

Brad quickly scooped Sarah up and held her in his arms. "Are you all right?" he asked, brushing her hair from her eyes.

Unable to speak just yet, she nodded her head, then sobbed on Brad's shoulder. Finally, she asked, "Can we go home now?"

Brad looked at the ghost, who had joined them on the bridge. "Can we?"

"Yes," said the ghost. "But first, follow me. I'll take you to the treasure. But we must hurry, for now that Zeena is dead, all her spells have been broken, and my spirit will soon be resting in peace."

The ghost led Brad and Sarah back to their quad, which now started up immediately. Then, riding double, the two of them followed the ghost to the witch's hut. There, they uncovered the buried treasure and loaded it onto the rack on the rear of the quad. Then they thanked the ghost for his help, and the ghost thanked *them* for freeing his soul.

Brad and Sarah watched sadly as the ghost slowly disappeared in the moonlight—never to be seen again.

With Zeena dead, and all her spells broken, Brad and Sarah had no trouble finding their way out of Wolverine Forest—even in the moonlit darkness. On the way home, Sarah used her cell phone to call her parents and let them know that she and Brad were all right. Then Sarah's parents called Brad's parents, and all four parents, along with police and rescue workers, met them on the road when they were only halfway home. It was a happy reunion, with tears of joy, and lots of hugs and kisses.

Everyone was shocked when Brad and Sarah showed them the treasure chest filled with thousands of gold and silver coins. "These coins are worth a fortune!" Brad's dad cried. "What are you kids going to do with the money?"

Brad blurted, "I'm going to buy a new qua-"

"We're going to build a school for the town of Wolverine," Sarah interrupted.

"Then, whatever's left over, Brad and I will split fifty-fifty." She shot a stern look at Brad and asked, "Agreed?"

Looking defeated, Brad nodded and said, "Yeah ... I agree."

And so the town of Wolverine finally got their very own school, and everyone was happy. And there was so much money left over, Brad and Sarah decided to turn Wolverine Forest into a wildlife park, where people, kids, and their families could go hiking and camping, and have parties and picnics. The town renamed Wolverine Forest, "The Tommy Hansen Nature Center," in honor of the little boy and his ghost, who helped defeat the wicked Zeena and her pet, Cytok. The townsfolk even placed a statue of little Tommy Hansen directly above the spot where Zeena's underground hut had been.

Now, day after day, dozens of children parade through the park with their parents, enjoying the beautiful woods and the wonderful wildlife.

And day after day, a baby creature with bone-white tusks lies hidden in the under-brush, watching … growing …

and waiting.